Published by: Turtleberry Press

Baltimore, Maryland

www.turtleberrypress.com

Both Sides of Me

By Turtleberry

No one ever said that starting over would be easy.

When Antoinette decided that she wanted more out of life, it was then and there that she realized she needed to leave the old her behind. Keeping her head down, she focused on grad school and her new job, making a conscious effort to do things differently so that she could see results she could be proud of. Unfortunately, a closed box still has cracks, and she quickly learns what can happen when her old life and new life collide.

Chapter One

I walked into the lunchroom and headed straight to the balcony. There was no point in paying attention to the women pretending their tables were full and the men trying to clear a space for me. That had been my life since middle school. Life as a small waist, big booty and breast having woman with naturally curly hair had prepared me for both the instant hatred and the instant lust. There was a part of me that thought it would change as an adult. I mean who would think that adults would be so childish, especially in the workplace? It was like that everywhere I went. I just hoped no one recognized me from social media.

After navigating through the crowded seating areas, I found an empty table outside. The breeze was nice but fall had set in. I put on my sweater before sitting down. As I began to pull some of my lunch out, I felt someone walking over to me. I looked over to see a guy coming closer.

"You're Antoinette?"

"Yes."

He sat a book down on the table. "You dropped this."

I looked down and realized it was my copy of *The Alchemist* that I had begun to read. "Oh. Wow. I didn't realize."

"Your name was on the letter you stuck in there."

"Thank you."

"You're welcome." He smiled at me and walked away.

For some reason I felt a little twinge of sadness that he didn't try to take that opportunity to prolong a conversation or try to shoot his shot like most guys would have. He was tall, had a beard, a nice smile, and pretty brown eyes. I almost let my eyes follow him as he went back inside. Then I remembered I was at work and focused back on my lunch. I really needed the job and workplace romances were landmines.

It took me three days to see him again and another day on top of that to figure out that his name was Wesley. I didn't want to ask anyone because that would mean that I was interested in him in some way. I didn't want to admit that to anyone, most importantly myself. Not that me thinking about him off and on since that first day wasn't a clue, at least to myself. Once I got down in the department that I was assigned to I found that he worked mostly in the department next door. The warehouse department, where we worked, was huge but my section was on the main travelling aisle. It was loud but I also got to do quite a bit of people watching.

There were a lot of interesting people at the warehouse. I tried to focus on them, and my job of course. However, I ended up focusing on Wesley. I saw him riding by on every piece of equipment there was. One night he was just across the aisle from my station in a lift that allowed him to reach the equipment at the ceiling, about two stories up. I did my best not to focus on him. I tried to focus on scanning and printing labels, which was so tedious and boring. It wasn't my dream job but it was necessary. I did my best to take it seriously and only steal glances at Wesley when I could get away with it.

After three weeks on the job my supervisor called me and told me that I was moving upstairs.

"Is this a good thing?"

He shrugged. "Get your stuff together and head up there. They want you to start now."

I headed over to my station and grabbed my bags. I only had my bookbag and lunch bag with me. The station was used by others during different shifts so I hadn't brought anything to personalize it. Once on the elevator I realized that I hadn't asked him specifically where upstairs I was supposed to report.

A woman smiled at me as the elevator doors opened. "Hi. You must be Antoinette."

"Yes."

"I'm Diane. Follow me. I will show you to your cubicle."

"Thank you."

I followed her down the hallway and to an open area I remembered from when I got hired. It was the Human Resources department. She showed me to a cubicle that was empty except for a computer, a chair, and a file cabinet.

"Okay this is where you will be. Your shift will stay the same. We're swamped with new hires and a ton of positions to hire for. I have ten people retiring just next month so we are grateful to have you up here. There will be two other people starting on this shift next week. Unfortunately, it is just you until then." She smiled at me. "I think you can handle it. The day shift has made a handbook of instructions for the things I need you to tackle tonight. If you need anything, I'm in the third office along this wall to your left."

"I have one question."

"Yes ma'am."

"How did I get picked for this position?"

Diane smiled. "Your shift manager thought this would be a better fit for you. We actually just posted this position last week so you wouldn't have seen it when you applied. I looked at your resume and you fit right in."

"He didn't seem happy to send me up here."

"Who? James? No, he was just your supervisor. Wesley Matthews is the shift manager down there."

My heart skipped a beat. "Oh. I think I met him once."

She nodded. "He's always busy. Hopefully we can send him the ten more people he needs down there."

I smiled and turned to the cubicle. "I guess I should get started then."

"Holler if you need me." Diane headed to her office.

I sat down at the desk and began to go over the instructions. In the back of my mind I wondered if I would get a chance to thank Wesley. Then I had to refocus back on my work before my mind went completely left.

I was sitting out on the balcony, eating my salad, while watching the sunset. It was chilly but beautiful and peaceful. It had been two weeks since I had moved upstairs. It was a great experience. I was studying Human Resources online during the day and my manager, Diane, was so helpful and was already encouraging me. Work and school were going great but my personal life was complete trash. I had worked part time while living with my boyfriend but when I discovered he was cheating on me I decided I needed a full-time job at night so I could save up to get my own place. The hardest part was he was happy to have me out of the house more.

"Don't you think it's too cold to be out here?"

I looked up to find Wesley standing at the side of my table. I smiled at him. "No. It's nice."

"Oh. Ok." He turned to walk away.

"Thank you."

"For?" He turned back.

"Diane told me you recommended me to go upstairs."

"Oh." He nodded. "You're welcome."

I wasn't sure what else to say so I looked out at the sunset.

"Did you finish reading *The Alchemist*?"

I looked up again. "Yes."

"Oh. Ok."

"Have you read it?"

"One of my favorites."

I pushed the chair next to me out. "What did you like the most?"

Wesley smiled. He sat down with me and we spent the rest of our lunch break talking about the book.

We hadn't eaten lunch together again. A week later he left a book, *The Four Agreements,* on my desk with a simple note saying that I would enjoy it. I wasn't sure when he dropped it off because I never saw him up there. I would see him in passing in the lunchroom. He would nod and I could see his eyes smiling, which gave me a warm feeling.

I found myself thinking about Wesley even more since our conversation. He was so eloquent. At times I felt he sounded more like a professor than a shift supervisor in a warehouse. It was a change of pace from my boyfriend who couldn't hold a three-minute conversation about anything other than basketball and questionable rap music. I wished that we could talk again but didn't know how to ask, having never needed to, and wasn't sure it was a good idea since we still worked for the same company.

Chapter Two

"Hey."

I stopped walking and turned around to face Wesley. My shift had just ended. "Hi."

"Are you… I mean would you…" Wesley looked away and then back at me.

I couldn't help but giggle. I had never imagined him stumbling over his words. "What's up?"

He looked around. "You parked this far?"

"I don't drive anymore."

"What happened?"

I looked away and then looked back. "I used to drive one of my boyfriend's cars. Can't really do that since I broke up with him and moved into my own place."

"Oh. Ok."

I smiled at his familiar response. "What were you going to ask me?"

"How about I give you a ride home and maybe I'll have the courage by the time we get there?"

I giggled. "That sounds like a plan."

Wesley led me back to his huge truck. He started it before we got close and opened the door so that I didn't even have to slow my stride. He reached out and took my backpack from me when I took it off my back. "Damn this is heavy."

"I was working on a paper during my down time."

"Must be nice to have down time." Wesley helped me up into the passenger seat.

I looked at him. "Well I wouldn't have any if some gentleman hadn't recommended I switch departments."

Wesley smiled. "True."

I put on my seatbelt and got comfortable. Wesley put my backpack in the backseat and then walked around the truck and got in. I got a good look at him before turning my head to look out the window. Wesley was entirely too good looking. He had soft edges to well defined features. I could feel his eyes on me as I tried not to run through everything about him that was so attractive. I leaned back in the seat. "These are heated too. I'm just going to let you type my address in GPS cause I might be going to sleep."

Wesley chuckled. "Okay. That works."

I looked down at my hands and gave Wesley my new address. "It's a brand-new complex."

"Those new apartments over near where they're building the new stadium?"

I nodded. "Huge discount because of the construction that's going on."

"Wow. How do you sleep through it?"

I shrugged. "I can sleep through the apocalypse if I'm tired enough."

"I would have thought you would live near the college."

"I don't go there."

"You don't?"

"Nope. I go to an online university." I sighed. "My ex was supportive of me going back to school but didn't want me on campus."

"I wonder why." Wesley glanced at me and then back at the road.

"Because he was screwing half of campus."

"Ouch. That isn't what I was thinking."

"What were you thinking?"

"I was thinking he might be insecure that you would get snatched up by someone else."

I turned to Wesley. "You know, he always joked about that and it's not that I didn't get offers even without going to that college. Hell, I got plenty of better offers but why would I get in a relationship if I wanted to play around. I'd just stay single and play around."

"Makes sense."

"Yet he wants to lock me down and proceeds to fuck every immature girl possible." I groaned. Then I took a deep breath. "Sorry. I shouldn't be fussing at you. It's just that I'm still getting messages from these girls who think they stole something from me."

Wesley put his hand on mine. "It's cool. Vent. Get it off your chest."

"I'm not gonna vent cause he doesn't deserve anymore of my breath." I glanced down and saw that Wesley's hand was still on top of mine. He must have noticed me noticing and he moved his hand. I looked back out the passenger side window. Then I looked down and saw a doll in the bin on the door. "You like to play with dolls?"

Wesley laughed as I held the doll up. "Naw. That belongs to one of my daughters."

"You have more than one?"

"Yes."

"Oh." I wanted to ask him more but didn't want to pry. I sat quietly and looked at the passing scenery. My body was full of nervous energy. There was a part of me that really wanted to kiss Wesley. Then there was another part scolding me from even having accepted the ride. Still another part wanted to ask him a million questions about his daughters and their mother and even more. My eyes went down to my hands and I scolded myself for barely being a month out of a relationship with one guy and so very interested in another.

"Did you want to borrow that one? I'm sure they won't miss it."

I looked up and realized that Wesley had pulled in front of my apartment building. Then I looked down at the doll. I had braided the doll's hair while I was trapped in my head. I smiled at Wesley. "No. It was kind of relaxing but I'm attempting this whole minimalist thing."

"So, you don't have any stuffed animals or anything?"

I rolled my eyes as Wesley chuckled. "I allowed myself one stuffed animal my grandfather got me when I was little. That's it for now."

"Oh. Okay." Wesley was quiet for a moment. Then he went to reach in the backseat. "I can get your bag for you..."

"What were you trying to ask me earlier?"

"Huh?" Wesley glanced back at me.

"Don't do that. You practically chased me down in the parking lot for a reason. What was the reason?"

Wesley sat my backpack in between us. Then he took a deep breath. "I noticed that you sometimes wear a Wonder Woman t-shirt. Well… I think you have more than one… not that I have been paying attention to what you wear… but…"

I giggled and opened my coat and jacket. I was wearing my favorite in my collection of Wonder Woman t-shirts. "Like this one?"

"Yes."

"Okay."

"So, I wanted to see if you wanted to go to the movies to see Justice League on Saturday night."

I smiled. "Yes. That sounds fun."

"Bet." Wesley licked his lips and nodded.

I was trying so hard not to kiss him so I opened the truck door. "Thanks for bringing me home."

"You're welcome. I can't imagine you on the bus this late."

"It's early. Not late." I pointed to the clock. It was four in the morning.

Wesley chuckled. "Good way of looking at it."

I started to get out of the car and then realized he didn't have my phone number. "Let me hold your phone."

He raised an eyebrow and then handed me his phone.

I typed my number in quickly and called my phone. I could feel it vibrating in my pocket so I disconnected the call. "There. I don't always see you at work so that way you can text me about Saturday night."

"Which apartment is yours?"

"Why?" I asked as hopped out of the truck.

"So, I know which light to look for. How else will I know you made it inside okay?"

I couldn't help but smile. I pointed to the balcony to the left of the door. "I'm just right there."

"Okay."

"Goodnight."

"You said it was early. Good morning."

I laughed and then shut the door. As I walked to the house my brain was at war with my hormones. I was sad that he didn't even try anything. I was also happy that he hadn't.

Most every guy I had ever been out with tried to come in, back to when I was fifteen. I tried not to look back at him in the truck when I opened my apartment door but I did notice that he inched up a bit to get a better view of me walking inside. After I got inside, I turned the light on and locked my door. Slowly I walked over to the patio door. Wesley was slowly pulling from in front of the building. I pulled my phone out and made sure to add him to my contacts. Then I went towards my bedroom, hoping I would be able to shower and stop thinking about Wesley long enough to sleep.

What should have been a fifteen-minute drive to his mother's house took twice that since Wesley couldn't get Antoinette off his mind. He missed two green lights due to his daydreaming and was thankful it was still before rush hour and his was practically the only car out there. He pulled into the huge circle driveway and parked in his usual spot. As he walked from the truck to the private entrance to his basement apartment, Wesley kept reminding himself that girls like Antoinette wouldn't be interested in him. She

was a smart college student with her own place. She also happened to be the most beautiful woman he had ever seen. Her curves made him dizzy. Wesley's dick got hard just at the memory of watching her perfect giant pear shaped ass walk up the few steps to her building. He walked in his apartment and headed straight for the shower.

After a quick shower and release of pressure, Wesley stood in the mirror with a towel around his waist. He did not lack self-esteem. He knew that he was an above average looking guy with a good job. He could hold a conversation on just about anything and had a nice sense of humor. The issue was his past and current situation. Wesley was living in the basement apartment at his mother's house. He had not one but three young daughters from a previous marriage. Those two facts were generally enough to scare a woman off. Scaring Antoinette off was the last thing he wanted to do. The first thing he wanted to do was wrap her legs around his waist. Wesley groaned at the thought and headed to his bed. He hoped he'd be able to sleep for a few hours before he had to get up and take his girls to school.

Three hours later, Wesley was up and making breakfast for the women in his life. His mother was the first in the kitchen. She was dressed in a suit and looked ready to tackle a day full of meetings.

"What is this I heard about you moving one of your clerks up to HR?" She poured her coffee and raised an eyebrow at him.

Wesley sighed. Working for the company his mother owned and ran was both a gift and a curse. She hated that he refused any of the office jobs he was overqualified for and decided to work in the warehouse. He typically couldn't do anything without the handful of people who knew he was her son reporting back to her. Frankly he was shocked that it had taken that long for her to hear about him moving Antoinette. "Yeah. That was a while ago. She belongs up there. I asked them to hire more people and they said they were short staffed."

"I heard that it was because she was a distraction."

Wesley chuckled. "The guys tended to be off task around her."

"Hmph." Mrs. Scott shook her head. "I'm not upset. They showed me her resume. A few of my HR people are nervous because she can take their jobs."

"Really." Wesley fixed his mother a plate. "I didn't pay that much attention to her resume."

"She's in graduate school, second to last semester. Don't be upset if she gets pulled to day shift."

"Why would I get upset?" Wesley was asking his mother but also asking himself because he instantly felt a little upset after she said it.

"I don't know." Mrs. Scott gave him the side eye and then began to eat her breakfast. "Go check on your girls. I think Carly was having a meltdown over her hair."

Wesley sighed. "I got it."

"Did Pat say she was still keeping them this weekend?"

"Yeah. She isn't sure she is up to the whole holiday thing this year so she was going to do a mini dinner with them tomorrow. I'm supposed to drop them off on my way to work tonight."

Mrs. Scott nodded. "Okay."

He paused in the doorway to see if she would add any of her usual commentary and was shocked by her silence.

Wesley turned and smiled at her before walking down the hallway. He went up the steps quickly and found his nine-year-old daughter, Carly, sitting on his youngest sister's bed. Michelle was putting Carly's hair in French braids.

"Daddy, why can't I get a relaxer?"

"Because neither your mother nor I want you to get one." He smiled at her and kept going down the hallway. He found his ten-year-old, Camryn, on her tablet. "Are you ready?"

"Yes."

"Then get your butt downstairs to the breakfast table." He went down one more door to find his eight-year-old, Corrine, taking selfies with her tablet in the bathroom. "This is why you can't have a phone."

"But..."

Wesley took the tablet and headed back down the hallway. "I'm leaving in twenty minutes whether y'all have had breakfast or not."

"Coming." Corrine yelled. She grabbed her backpack from the floor and ran down the hallway.

Wesley stepped to the side to let her head down the steps. Camryn and Carly were right behind her. He shook his head when Michelle came out of her room with her briefcase.

Michelle smiled at him. "What time did y'all get done last night?"

"Quarter to four."

"Wow. I guess those few extra people really made a difference."

"I told you they would." Wesley followed Michelle down the steps.

"I heard you but you know your brother is all about lowering operating expenses."

"Yet he gets pissed when the trucks aren't ready to go out first thing in the morning."

She sighed. "You should really come up to the office. Greg needs to spend more time lightening mom's load."

"Mom would have to let him."

"She's getting tired of his shit." Michelle shrugged and then got quiet as she walked into the kitchen.

Their mother was giving each of the girls some eggs. Wesley walked over and took the pot from her when she was finished. "Ma, I got it."

"I'm fine." She smiled at him.

"Daddy, can we stay home this weekend? I wanted to go to the movies with you." Camryn frowned.

"Nope. You ladies are spending time with your mom this weekend and we will do the movies next weekend if she doesn't take you."

"She won't take us." Carly shook her head. "She doesn't like crowds and dark places and…"

"And I don't like what you're saying out of your mouth so fill it with some bacon and eggs so we can go and I can go to bed." Wesley leaned against the wall. He hated when his girls acted like they didn't want to see their mother. Patricia had been doing well lately with her depression and he wanted them to enjoy the time. She typically wasn't doing well during the holidays so Wesley was worried things would shift and the girls wouldn't get time with her. He sighed as Corrine tugged on his arm. "Yes ma'am?"

"I'm ready to go. Can we take the new truck?"

He smiled at his baby girl. "If you insist."

She grinned. "I do."

I changed my clothes six times before settling on a sweater and a pair of corduroy pants. Wesley had said we would go to the movies and get something to eat afterward. I wasn't sure how laid back I should dress. I knew he had seen me in the jeans and leggings I always wore to work so I decided to do something just a little bit different. I had a brand-new Wonder Woman clutch that I planned on carrying with the outfit. His text telling me he was ten minutes away set my nerves a blaze. I put what I needed in the clutch, put on my small peacoat, and was out of my apartment. I waited by the front door to the building.

Wesley pulled up a few minutes later. He looked like he was going to park but then he saw me. He pulled up in front of the door and got out of the truck. He smiled at me as I came out of the building. "I would have rung the bell."

"I know." I shifted my weight. "I got ready a little early."

"Okay." Wesley reached for my hand. When I placed it in his, he led me to his truck. "There is a movie starting in a half hour. We can see the movie first and then eat or the other way around."

"Movie first is fine." I climbed in the truck.

We headed over to the theater. I was glad to see that Wesley was a popcorn eater. He got a jumbo popcorn and we each got a soda. Wesley kept the popcorn in his lap but he wasn't greedy with it. I didn't even notice him eating it until I saw that it was completely empty when the movie was over.

"What was that end scene about?" I fussed while we walked out of the theater. "They're not Marvel. Why are they trying to be Marvel?"

"I can't even begin to tell you."

"And Ben Affleck is not Batman." I groaned.

"He isn't the worst Batman."

"Naw." I said quickly. "Val Kilmer was the worst Batman. That isn't even a contest."

Wesley laughed. "Who was your favorite?"

"Michael Keaton. He was great as both Bruce Wayne and Batman. George Clooney was a great Bruce Wayne. Christian Bale was a great Batman."

"I'm a Christian Bale Batman fan."

"Wonder Woman was good in this. Aquaman was good to look at." I smiled.

Wesley shook his head and held the theater door open for me. "What would you like to eat?"

"I could really go for some wings but this sweater is not wing appropriate."

"Okay."

"There is a spot down the street that has some really good sweet and spicy chicken tenders."

"Oh, that sounds like a plan." I waited for Wesley to open the truck door before I climbed in.

Our conversation continued in the car. We talked about all the superhero movies we had seen. Over dinner the discussion shifted to movies in general. There were a bunch of movies that we decided that the other had to watch. I felt so relaxed with Wesley. I was not usually that relaxed on first dates. Wesley was so easy to talk to. I was sad when he pulled up in my complex. I wanted to ask him to come up but his phone began to ring.

"Shit." Wesley groaned and then answered the call.

I could tell simply from his side of the conversation that the call was from work. When he hung up, I raised my eyebrow. "Is everything okay?"

"Nope." Wesley put his head on the steering wheel for a moment. Then he looked at me. "One of the guys backed a forklift into an almost empty set of shelves that I told someone to bolt to the floor two days ago."

"Let me guess." I paused. "They weren't bolted to the floor."

"Bingo."

"Was anyone hurt?"

"No." Wesley took a deep breath and then smiled at me. "Well, we know what I'm about to be doing. What about you?"

"I have a paper to finish." I touched his hand. "Text or call me when you are done. I'll still be up."

"Okay."

I leaned over and kissed Wesley on the cheek. I wanted to kiss him on the lips but they looked so good I knew I would try and keep him from going to work. "Don't forget to text me."

"I won't forget."

Chapter Three

Diane came over to my cubicle and smiled at me. It was the smile she always gave me when she was going to ask me to do something more than what she asked the other two girls who worked overnight to do. I had learned quickly that those girls were only there because they didn't want to do the hard work that was done in the warehouse. They really didn't want to do the HR work either. Diane hated working overnight but it was the only way she could get a promotion. She was so thankful that I didn't mind doing extra and I also would pop in her office to make sure she was staying awake.

"Toni, the HR director wants you to take a certification class."

"Like a class I have to go and sit in?"

"No." She smiled. "It is a bunch of online modules. I did it a year ago. It's a lot of reading and remembering but the actual class only takes two days to complete."

I looked at the papers she gave me. I had heard of the certification. A few of my online classmates already had it. I looked up at her and smiled. "Okay."

"I'm not sure how you will do that and the other stuff you have to do but…"

"I'll figure it out." I knew she was saying that for the benefit of my nosey coworkers who were likely listening from their cubicles. Diane already knew that I got my work done during the first four hours of my eight hours shift and spent the rest of my time studying.

"Good. They still expect you to keep up with that as well." Diane smiled and then walked over to one of my coworker's cubicles.

Shana looked at her. "Are we doing that certification thing as well?"

"No. It requires you to already have a degree." Diane shook her head. "Besides, I offered to send you both to that training last month and you both turned me down."

The other girl groaned. "It was a two-week class during the day."

Diane sighed and walked back to her office without saying another word.

Before either one of them could make their way to my cubicle, I put my headphones on and logged in to the website that Diane had just given me. After reading through all the introductions and instructions, I knew that I would have it finished before the holiday. Most of the modules were things I had learned the semester prior. Being in my last semester of grad school was definitely an advantage. I got through three modules before lunchtime.

Typically, I ate lunch at my desk but that day I decided to go down to the cafeteria and see what they had. I was looking around when I saw Shana talking to Wesley. I had to turn to hide my snicker. Wesley looked like he was desperately trying to get away from her. I saw my other coworker, Keisha, attempting to sneak into the stairwell with one of Wesley's floor supervisors. I glanced back at Shana and Wesley. She had moved closer to him and was touching his arm. My heart started to race and my face felt a little hot. I could feel the jealousy bubbling inside of me so I grabbed a premade salad and walked over to the register. The company gave us all free food within certain parameters so all I had to do was swipe my badge. Then I headed back over to the elevators.

I wasn't sure if Wesley saw me until I got back to my desk and saw a new text message on my phone.

Wes: Where did you run off to?

Me: My desk. I don't care much for the crowd down there.

Wes: Why didn't you save me from her?

Me: LOL. Aren't you in charge? Can't you just send her away to go do work?

Wes: I'm not her boss.

Me: Oh.

Wes: Part of the reason I had you moved up there.

Me: Interesting.

Wes: Are you going to sneak out of here like you did Friday night?

Me: I thought you didn't notice.

Wes: I just didn't mention.

Me: I'm fine. I can take the bus.

Wes: You are indeed fine. I just can't deal with you on the bus in the middle of the night.

Me: What if people see me leaving with you and start talking?

Wes: Zero fucks given.

Me: I gotta get back to this thing Diane has me doing.

I put my phone face down on the desk and didn't look at Wesley's response. He clearly didn't seem concerned about what people thought. I was still nervous that would mess things up at a job I actually liked.

Shana came upstairs and smirked at me. "All the hotties work in the warehouse. I wish we could go down there more often. I almost had Wesley's number but he got called back to the loading dock."

I put my headphones back on and returned to the training modules. There was no way I could stomach listening to Shana talk about her attempt to holler at Wesley.

Wesley walked down the administrative hallway to check his mailbox. He had one down on the warehouse level but his mother insisted on him also having one up on the administrative hallway. Diane was in the mailroom when he walked in. The scowl on her face had him turning around to leave.

"Nope. Don't you try to run."

"What did I do now?"

"Did you send that girl up to take my job?"

"Huh?"

"Toni. Did you send Toni up to take my job?"

"Of course not." Wesley took the pile of papers out of his mailbox. "I barely looked at her resume. My mom said she is getting her master's degree."

"Yes."

"Aren't you doing that as well?"

Diane huffed and leaned against the copy machine. "Yes. But with these night hours I'm too tired to go more than part time. Toni is in her last semester."

"Oh. I didn't know that."

"Greg was talking about your mother wanting her on day shift and they have her getting that certification they require."

"Oh. Shit." Wesley sighed. He had hoped his mother was kidding with her comment. "Well, who's to say that Toni will want to work the day shift."

"She said she likes the night shift last time I asked her." Diane looked at the door and then whispered. "She keeps me awake."

Wesley smiled. "See that is a good thing."

"She does great work; unlike the two nitwits I have working with her." Diane groaned. "They're going to give her that day shift promotion because she's more qualified."

"Diane, stop tripping. You have been with the company for like five years."

"Six."

"You have the time in. My mom values that more than education."

"Whatever." Diane rolled her eyes. "Your little girlfriend is going to take my promotion."

"If she was my girlfriend, why in the hell would I want her on a different shift?"

Diane paused. Then she raised her hand. "Maybe your mom doesn't want you dating her."

Wesley started to say something but decided not to get baited. "Whatever."

"Well, no matter. Shana was bragging loud as hell that she almost got your number and how you look at her. I'm sure Toni heard it all over the headphones she has on." Diane took her papers off the copy machine that had just stopped. "Look, I like Toni. I just..."

"I'll see what is up with them. I highly doubt they're going to promote Toni ahead of you."

"Thanks. I hate to have a favor I did for you come back to bite me in the ass."

"Naw. Never that. Biting you in the ass is Ted's job." Wesley chuckled. Diane's husband, Ted, previously worked for the company before taking a different job.

"He doesn't get time with these crazy ass hours I keep."

"Let me see what I can find out."

"Okay." Diane headed to the door. "Toni gets off at three tonight. Shana gets off at two."

Wesley chuckled. "I'll keep that in mind."

Wesley tried to allow himself to let Antoinette take the bus home. He watched her walk across the parking lot and through the gate, thinking he could do it. Then he shook his head and started his truck. The bus stop was not in full view of the building but the security guard could see it from his gate. Wesley waved to him as he pulled out. Then he pulled up at the bus stop. He watched Antoinette roll her eyes and he got nervous. Then she smiled, got up from the bench, and walked over to his truck.

She was quiet while she put on her seat belt and then she turned to him. "You just couldn't..."

"Nope."

Her smile warmed him more than the seat warmer did. "I was thinking about getting a car next month."

Wesley started driving down the street. "Graduation present to yourself?"

"How do you know I'm graduating?"

"Diane told me."

"Oh." Antoinette looked down at her hands and smiled. "She's so sweet. She keeps encouraging me. Then tonight, she showed me some job announcements for other companies."

"Oh."

"It came from out of the blue. She just sat them on my desk and then went upstairs to the administrative wing to make copies when we have a copy machine." Antoinette shook her head. "I'm so confused. I hope she doesn't think I'm going to try to take her job."

"You don't want her job?"

"I mean, if it means she gets a promotion then maybe." Antoinette leaned back. "It has taken me this long to figure out what she does."

Wesley laughed. "Really?"

"The organizational chart on the internal website is a piece of shit. The director of HR has no clue what he's doing. I swear." She shook her head. "And I try not to listen to the gossip but I heard he works for his mom and is really supposed to be running the money side of things."

"Is that what you heard?"

"Yes. Keisha gets her info from…" Antoinette covered her mouth and then looked out the window. "Now I'm a gossip."

Wesley laughed. "I won't think any less of you."

Antoinette glanced back at Wesley for a moment and then looked away. "Anyway, he's horrible at HR. Diane could really whip things into shape with some help."

"Help like you?"

"Maybe."

"Why don't you want day shift?"

"I dunno. Maybe I like occasionally bumping into you."

Wesley was pleasantly surprised by her revelation. "Well, I know I like bumping into you."

"I just don't want there to be any problems at work."

"What if I promise there won't be any problems at work?"

Antoinette was quiet for a while. Then she turned and smiled at Wesley when he pulled in front of her building. "You can't promise that."

"I can."

"But it's out of your control to keep it."

"Okay." Wesley sighed.

"Don't make promises you can't keep just because you want to kiss me."

Wesley chuckled. "How do you know I want to kiss you?"

"It's in your eyes." Antoinette took off her seatbelt and leaned across the truck. She kissed Wesley softly on the lips and then sat back.

Her lips were a lot softer than Wesley had imagined. "I could get addicted to that."

Antoinette smiled. "But you need to go home and get some sleep before you have to take your girls to school."

"I have three."

"Three?"

"Three daughters." Wesley braced for her shock but her smile never faded.

"I bet you're an awesome dad. I mean, you don't care if your car is filled with dolls."

Wesley chuckled. "It's just the glitter that drives me crazy."

"Glitter is great."

"It's horrible. It gets everywhere and never leaves."

Antoinette laughed. "It does so leave. Otherwise I'd be covered in it."

Wesley raised his eyebrow and imagined Antoinette covered in glitter. "Um..."

She smacked him in the arm. "I'm going inside. Text me when you get home."

"I will." Wesley watched Antoinette get out of the truck and head inside her building. He waited until she got in the apartment, and saw her light go on, before he drove off. This time, Wesley was paying attention and made it home in fifteen minutes. He pulled his phone out to text Antoinette as soon as he walked in his door.

Me: I made it home safely.

Toni: That was quick. Were you speeding?

Me: LOL Naw. I don't actually live that far from you.

Toni: I'm glad. I was worried I took you too far out of your way.

Me: Wouldn't matter if you did.

Toni: I gotta get a car soon.

Me: Or I can just keep bringing you home after work every night hoping to get a goodnight kiss.

Toni: Wes…

Me: You'd save a fortune on car insurance that way.

Toni: Boy, go to bed. LOL

Me: Goodnight beautiful

Toni: Goodnight cutie

Me: Oh. You think I am cute?

Toni: Boy bye!

Wesley chuckled and then sighed just before collapsing on his bed.

"Yes. I was hoping to move Antoinette up to the day shift to replace Sheila when she retires."

Wesley groaned. "Ma, why? What about Diane?"

"I thought about Diane but Greg said that Antoinette has the better resume."

"How?" Wesley huffed in frustration. "Diane has been with the company for six years."

"But she doesn't have her master's degree."

"Greg has two and is a damn idiot."

Michelle snickered and her mother shot her a glance. Then Mrs. Scott turned to Wesley. "Well if you think you know better then maybe you should run it so Greg can get back to what you feel he is best at."

"He's best at working my damn nerve." Wesley mumbled under his breath, causing his mother to smack him on the arm. "Listen, I might have a plan."

"Does it involve you coming upstairs to work with us?" Michelle asked.

"Nope." Wesley smiled. "I'm most effective in the warehouse."

"Why do you want Diane promoted and Antoinette not?" Mrs. Scott leaned against the island and sipped her coffee.

"I want them both promoted. I just know that Diane has busted her ass for the company and if you bypass her she might just quit." Wesley turned as his daughters ran into the kitchen. "Ladies, good morning. We're late so it is breakfast bars and fruit. Grab it and let's go."

"I want your plan on my desk Monday morning or we're going to consider Greg's plan."

"No you're not, cause you know I'm right. Talk to Sheila and see what she says." Wesley kissed his mother on the cheek. "Don't forget I'm closing the warehouse Friday night."

Mrs. Scott groaned. "Why?"

"Um… it's my birthday Saturday and I don't want to work. Doug is throwing that party."

"So, we are shut down for two nights?"

"Yes. Orders will be fine. We're caught up."

"But Greg said…"

Wesley held the door open for his girls. He unlocked the doors and started the car with his remote. "Greg hasn't been on my warehouse floor in three years. He has no clue what goes on down there."

"Ma, we will be fine. They come back Saturday night." Michelle added.

Mrs. Scott sighed. "Get my girls to school on time without speeding."

"Yes ma'am." Wesley chuckled and shut the door.

"Hey." Diane came over and leaned against the file cabinet in my cubicle.

"I thought you left early."

"Nope. Trying to get some things done so Monday won't be super crazy."

"Oh." I smiled.

"So. I was talking with Wesley, and don't be mad at him but he said that you might have some ideas to help this place run more efficiently."

I looked down at my keyboard. "I was just talking… I mean…"

"Listen, my boss is retiring at the end of the year."

"Mr. Sampson is old enough to retire?"

Diane laughed. "I wish."

I chuckled. "Oh."

"Sheila Dennis is my boss. She is the actual head of HR. Greg Sampson is just second in command to his mother. He's attempting to help out but…"

"He has a lane he needs to stay in."

"Exactly." Diane smiled. "This place is going to be nuts with Sheila gone. She's already only part time because her Lupus is acting up. That is why we are struggling so badly. I have ideas but I was hoping that we could put our heads together."

I smiled. "I don't have your level of experience."

"But you have fresh eyes and probably some really good ideas." Diane pulled over a chair. "Tweddle Dee and Tweddle Dumb are already gone so let's hear what you got."

Diane and I spent the next hour going over all my ideas for changes that would make the company run more efficiently from an HR standpoint. She stopped me when I suggested that she step in as the day shift HR lead. "You don't want to go for that position?"

"No. I've always been a night owl." I thought back to my undergraduate years and how hard it was to stay awake in class. "I have worked night shift and overnight shift since my sophomore year."

"Oh." Diane smiled. "Okay. Well, I can write this up and present it to them on Monday."

"Do you think they will even listen?"

"Wesley is listening."

I looked away. "Yeah."

Diane stood up. "You should pack up and get out of here. I saw you passed the certification in record time. You're going to make the rest of us look bad."

"You, no." I laughed. "Those two don't make it hard to make them look bad."

"Well, I can tell you one thing. Those two won't be here long. Their type doesn't stay."

"Really?"

"Shana is a party girl." Diane paused. "Not that there's anything wrong with that. She just isn't good at it. Every time I ask her about her future goals, she has nothing. Keisha says she wants to move up to be a supervisor but won't take any of my suggestions."

"Oh."

"You're a hard worker and industrious. I can tell even though we haven't worked together very long." Diane smiled at me. "Pack up. Go home and enjoy your holiday."

"Are we really off Friday?"

"Yup. Wesley is in charge over the holiday and he shut this whole place down." Diane took her papers and headed to her office. "See you Monday evening."

"See you then. Enjoy your holiday."

I finished up what I was working on and then packed up my things. I sent Wesley a text but he didn't respond. I decided to head down to the warehouse floor and see how long he was going to be. When I got down there I saw that they were extremely busy.

"Let's get this shipment ready. I'm trying to get y'all out of here." Wesley's voice came over the loudspeaker.

I sighed and walked over to my old section. There was one young lady printing labels. "Where is everyone?"

"Three people called out and the rest were scheduled off." She groaned. "This is the worst part of the job. It's usually just me until they get done in the other section. Then people come over to help."

"Want some help?" I sat my bag on the table.

"You don't mind? I mean, this isn't your job."

"It used to be." I smiled at her.

"Okay. Cool." She handed me a scanner.

The young lady and I worked together and got caught up in thirty minutes. I showed her a much more efficient way to do her job in the process. She jumped when she heard Wesley yelling.

"What's wrong?"

"He hates me."

I shook my head. "No. I'm sure he doesn't hate you."

"He's always yelling."

"Y'all need to hurry up so you can help Nina with this backlog." Wesley yelled as he walked into her work area.

"Stop yelling. There is no backlog." I put my hand on my hip. "Nina is on top of things."

Wesley stood there, speechless for a moment. Then he smiled at Nina. "Good job drafting help. I'm sending over a few people so you can go ahead and take your last break."

Nina leaned over to me when she walked past. "Thank you."

I winked at her. Then I looked at Wesley. "Clearly you need a few more people down here."

"Just one for this section. We're trying to clear two nights worth of work so we won't be behind when we come back on Saturday." Wesley leaned against the pillar. "You waiting for me?"

"I don't have to. I can catch the bus."

"No you won't." Wesley chuckled. "Did you want to hide out in my office?"

"Nope. I can help you guys finish."

"Cool."

We all worked for another hour and the horn sounded that the shipment was ready to go. I finished off the last of the labels and let Nina pack up. Then I headed to hide in Wesley's office. His door was open and he was down the hall, talking with the other supervisors. He came into his office ten minutes later.

I sighed at how tired he looked. "You look too sleepy to drive."

"Naw. I'm good." He yawned. "You just have to talk to me."

I nodded. "I can do that."

"Start by telling me what you're doing for the holiday."

"I was going to go to my grandmother's but my cousin is being difficult and I don't think I can be bothered with him." I groaned as Wesley locked his office and we headed to the side exit. "I wanted to come back Friday morning but I made the mistake of telling my cousin I was off. He doesn't want to drive up here again until Saturday. I'm out of his way and he's annoying."

"How far does your grandmother live?"

"Almost two hours from here."

"Wow."

"I used to visit every Saturday." I shrugged. "Another reason why I can't wait to get a car."

"Ah." Wesley yawned and then hit the button on his keychain to start his truck.

I saw how his eyes were barely open. "Maybe I should drive."

"You can drive this big truck?"

"Yes." I rolled my eyes at him.

"Go for it. I can close my eyes for a few minutes and then take my ass home to bed."

"Okay." I climbed in the driver's seat. I adjusted the seat while Wesley got in.

"You good?"

"Yup."

"Cool."

I pulled off after adjusting the mirrors. Wesley's legs were so long compared to mine. I glanced at him after waving to the security guard when he opened the gate for me. Wesley was already knocked out. I sighed and continued to my place. I took my time to try and let Wesley get as much of a nap as possible. When we got to my complex, I nudged him. He opened his eyes but then shut them again. I did it twice more and got the same result. Finally, I just parked his truck in the reserved space I never used.

I got out and walked over to the passenger side. After opening the door, I leaned in and kissed Wesley softly on the lips. As expected, he opened his eyes. I smiled. "We're at my place. You're way too sleepy to drive. Why don't you come in and get a nap before you go home?"

"I'm good."

"Nope. I'll be worried sick. I saw a picture of your girls in your office. They want you home in one piece."

Wesley closed his eyes for a moment and then opened them again. "Okay. Fine."

He got out and locked his car. Then I took his hand and led him to my apartment. "Did you not sleep before work?"

"Naw. Mom was off and my sister wasn't so I had to take her to the store to get food. Then the girls kept me up when they got out of school."

"Damn. So, you got how much sleep?"

"Three hours."

I opened my apartment door. "That isn't good."

"I'll just nap on your couch real quick."

I looked in my empty living room. "I don't have a couch."

"Oh."

"Gimme your coat." I hung my coat up in the closet and then hung Wesley's on the closet door. I couldn't help but giggle. He was like a big, half sleep kid. He rubbed his eyes and yawned. I took his hand again. "Come on."

He followed me into my bedroom. "I can sleep on the floor."

"You can lay down on that bed and take a nap is what you can do." I pointed to the bed. Then I went into the bathroom. When I came back out, Wesley was passed out on the far side of my bed. I went into my hope chest and pulled out a blanket to cover him up. Then I went to shower.

Waking up next to Antoinette threw Wesley off. It took him a moment to remember what had happened and how he got there. He got up and went into her bathroom. He had to splash some water on his face and mentally tell his dick to calm down.

"Now is not the time son." Wesley pulled his phone out of his pocket and checked the time. It was almost eight. He called his sister.

"Where are you? I don't see your truck."

"I'm at a friend's house." He paused. "Can you come and get me?"

"Why? What's wrong with your truck?"

"Nothing. I'm going to let her borrow it so she can go have dinner with family."

"Oh. I wanna know who she is."

"So, then I guess that means you're going to come and get me and then I will tell you."

"Okay." Michelle paused. "Mom and the girls are already up and in the kitchen."

"Don't bring the girls."

"I won't. Besides, they're making pie."

"Okay. I'll text you the address." Wesley hung up and sent his text. Then he splashed more water on his face and rinsed his mouth out with some mouthwash.

Stepping back into the bedroom, he had to remind his dick to calm down. Antoinette was asleep with one leg hanging out over the blanket. He could see she was wearing nothing but a t-shirt and a thong. He cursed himself for being so quick to call his sister. Then he remembered his plan. Wesley pulled his phone back out and took a quick picture of Antoinette. Something told him he wouldn't be able to get the image out of his mind but he didn't want to chance it. He walked over to the bed and sat next to Antoinette. He decided to wake her up the same way she woke him up in the car a few hours earlier. It took one kiss for her to stir, a second for her to put her arms around his neck, and a third for her to open her eyes. Wesley moved her arms but held her hands when he sat back.

"Good morning."

"Did you get enough rest?" She smiled.

"Yes. Thank you."

"So I don't have to worry about you crashing into a pole?"

Wesley chuckled. "Not at all because my sister is on her way to pick me up."

"Why?"

Wesley reached in his pocket and put his keys in her hands. "I want you to borrow my truck and go visit your grandmother."

"Really?"

"Yes."

"But..."

Wesley put his finger over her lips. "Hush. Stay overnight and come back tomorrow. Enjoy yourself and time with your grandmother."

"Won't you need your car?"

"I have another one. Brand new one actually."

Antoinette shook her head. "Wes…"

He kissed her softly as his phone buzzed in his pocket. "Saved by the text. I gotta get out of here cause you are too damn fine."

She smiled at him. "I can walk you to the door."

"Naw. Cause if you get up I will lose all the willpower I have and my sister will have to kick my ass." Wesley stood up and took her in with his eyes one more time. "Text me so I know you're safe and having fun and whatnot."

"Okay. I'll be back by two tomorrow."

"Maybe you can come with me to this whack ass party I have to go to."

Antoinette giggled. "Okay."

"Go back to sleep." Wesley headed out to the front door. He grabbed his coat from off the closet door and left out of the apartment, locking the door behind him.

Michelle was sitting out front. She raised her eyebrow when Wesley got in her car. "So…"

"I'm letting Toni borrow my truck so she can go see her grandmother. I was exhausted after work and she let me crash for a minute."

"Well I'm glad you didn't fall asleep behind the wheel." Michelle pulled off. "And I'm glad that you have a friend. I hear she's really nice."

"She is."

"Maybe I will get to meet her outside of work."

Wesley chuckled. "I invited her to the party tomorrow night."

"Nice." Michelle paused. "Wait, didn't you say that it was going to be whack?"

"I hope it won't. Doug said it's looking bleak."

"No one told him to break up with his girlfriend while he was trying to launch his new club." Michelle shook her head. "That girl did all the work."

"Well, we'll see what happens. If it's horrible that's just the excuse I need to leave with Toni."

"Did you tell her it's your birthday?"

"Nope."

"Wes..."

"I'll tell her. I just had to get out of there. She was in a t-shirt and thong and lawd..." Wesley groaned.

Michelle chuckled. "You must really have wanted her to see her family."

"She doesn't have a car. She used to drive her ex's car. She said she hasn't visited in a while."

"You're such a sweetie." Michelle paused. "Does she know about the girls?"

"Yup."

"And she didn't run?"

"Nope."

"What about work?"

"Naw." Wesley shook his head. "Greg and mom having a different last name has thrown her off a bit. I'll have to tell her about that too if things progress the way they are progressing."

"I'm excited for you." Michelle pulled up in the driveway. "Mom said you went past the house yesterday."

"Yeah. It'll be ready before Christmas."

"Moving out. Getting a girlfriend." Michelle sniffed. "I'm proud of you big brother."

"Oh Jesus. I'm going to bed. Tell mom I'll be up after a nap."

"You'll be up when your daughters wake you up."

"Truth." Wesley chuckled.

Chapter Four

"Okay young lady. Who does that truck in my driveway belong to?" My grandmother sat down in the rocker on her back porch.

"It belongs to a friend."

"What's his name?"

I sighed. "Wesley."

"How long have you known him?"

"A few months. We work together."

"Yet you haven't mentioned him when we talk on the phone."

"Grammy..."

"That tells me you're nervous and you really like him." She smiled at me.

I couldn't help but grin. "He's different."

"Different how, baby?"

"He's smart. Like he could be a professor smart but he runs the warehouse at my job."

"Nothing wrong with that."

"No. It doesn't bother me at all. He's older than me."

"How much older?" Grammy raised her eyebrow.

"I think he is around 30 or so. I work in HR and it is so hard not to go and look in his file even though I have access."

"Good girl. No cheating."

I giggled. "He told me about his kids."

"He has kids?"

"Three daughters. He was married before I think."

"Y'all haven't talked about it?"

"No. We went out on one date. I've been nervous about us working together but he says it isn't a big deal."

"Is it against the rules?"

"No. He moved me from his section so I don't work for him at all."

"Smart man." Grammy smiled. "When's your next date?"

"He invited me to a party tomorrow night."

"Is he better than the last one?"

"I think so Grammy." I looked down at my ringing phone and gasped. "I forgot to text him and tell him I got here safe."

"Oh well you better answer that." Grammy got up. "I need to go and stir these greens. Dinner will be ready in an hour."

"Okay." I sighed and answered Wesley's call. "I'm sorry."

"I woke up to no text and decided to call you before I freaked out."

I giggled. "No freaking out. I got here an hour ago. I meant to text you but Grammy put me to work and then my annoying ass cousin started talking to me. I just escaped to the back porch."

"I was sleeping until my daughters decided it was time for me to get up."

"Your own personal alarm clock."

"Three very loud ones. They decided to come and watch television in my room."

"Is it almost dinner time for you guys?"

"Two hours, maybe. My sister's husband just surprised her and that halted all cooking."

"Surprises are nice."

"This one was. He's in the Army. She didn't think he was going to get leave." Wesley paused. "She's living here too while he's deployed."

"Wow. How big is your mom's house?"

"Huge." Wesley sighed. "But not big enough. I hope to be out of here by the end of the year."

"Really?"

"Yeah. Can't live in my mom's basement for the rest of my life."

I laughed. "Nothing wrong with that. You're probably helping her out."

"If you consider dumping the trash and dealing with repair people helping out. That's all she lets me do. Oh, and I can fix breakfast and make her coffee."

"See. You're helping."

Wesley chuckled. "I have been helping for a while. She's ready for her house back."

"Your sister will still be there for a bit though."

"Naw. Michelle is coming with me. Fred's deployment has at least another ten months, I think. She is the one who really helps me with the girls."

"Oh."

"My mom did a lot when I first got divorced. But once Michelle moved home, she passed the baton."

I smiled listening to him talk about his family. I leaned back and glanced at my family through the picture window. They were inside arguing about something.

"Is that an argument?"

"Oh you can hear that?" I laughed. "My family is loud as shit."

"I can see why you're on the porch." Wesley chuckled.

Grammy opened the screen door. "Toni, baby, you mind picking up the twins from the bus station since your cousin Bernard is being an ungrateful piece of..."

"Grammy don't start cursing. Last time you went off for an hour and got your pressure up." I fussed.

"First he didn't want to pick you up and now he thinks he's going to sit his wide ass at my dinner table after telling me he won't pick up his own siblings from the bus station..."

"Half siblings." Bernard hollered from in front of the television.

Grammy took the towel off her hip. "Boy..."

"Oh shit." I covered my mouth and turned to look in the window.

"What's happening?" Wesley asked.

"Grammy is in the living room hitting my cousin Bernard with her dish towel."

"You should go pick up whoever she asked you to."

"You sure? I don't want to use your truck as a taxi service."

Wesley chuckled. "And I don't want your Grammy whipping your ass with her dish towel."

"Good point." I got up and went inside to get my purse. "I'll be back. Y'all better calm Grammy down or we won't eat."

Wesley chuckled in my ear. "Your family sounds hilarious."

"We are if you aren't a part of it." I climbed up in his truck. "Okay. How do I switch you to speaker?"

Wesley talked me through connecting my phone to his truck. Then he groaned.

"What's wrong?"

"I closed my eyes and had a flashback of you this morning. Lawd, girl do you know how fine you are?"

I laughed. "Thank you."

"I mean you know how hard it was for me to leave you there in that little ass t-shirt and you had your leg out..." Wesley groaned again.

"I had to put something on. I didn't want you to be uncomfortable if you woke up and I was naked. I don't usually sleep in clothes."

"Um… for future reference you would not make me uncomfortable. It's your house. You be as comfortable as you want." Wesley paused. "Neither one of us would have made it to dinner though."

I laughed again. "You're silly."

"I'm honest."

"I appreciate you letting me use your truck to come and see my Grammy."

"You're welcome. I'm glad to help." Wesley paused. "You can borrow my truck whenever you want to go visit."

"Don't say that. I like to visit her every week. You're going to get sick of me until I get a car."

"Never."

I smiled. "Well I will have your truck back to you by two tomorrow."

"Actually, I was hoping you would just hold onto it and meet me at this party that I cannot get out of going to."

"Why can't you get out of going? Why would you want to get out of it?"

"It is a dual birthday party my cousin is throwing at this club he bought with his inheritance."

"Oh. I'm sorry someone died."

"Yeah, my grandfather."

"Oh I'm really sorry to hear that."

"It was a year ago. He was mean as shit. I'm over it."

I tried to hold in my laughter. "Wes…"

"What? Sorry, more honesty." Wesley sighed. "I'm having a house built and he buys a club."

"His priorities are different."

"Obviously." Wesley paused.

"So, is it his birthday?"

"His is Friday and mine is Saturday."

"Oh. Well then you should go."

"And you should come with me."

I laughed. "Okay. I can do that. I haven't been to a party in a while actually."

"This is going to be bad though."

"Why do you keep saying that?"

"He wants to be a promoter and have great stuff at his club but he had his girlfriend doing all the work."

"Work?"

"Networking and promotions."

"So?" I paused. "Wait, he didn't break up with her, did he?"

"Bingo."

I groaned. "Rookie mistake."

"So now she has gone on social media bashing his club and he doubts anyone is even going to show up." Wesley sighed. "He's up in the living room crying into a beer."

"Wes, you gotta help him. What's she saying?"

"I don't know. I'm not on social media."

"Why not?"

"Never interested me."

"Oh." I was quiet.

"Are you on social media?"

"Not as much as I used to be." I grinned. I wasn't lying. I just was avoiding the truth.

"So, I can send you his info and you can see for yourself. My sister tells me it's bad."

"Okay. You want me to share the flyer, maybe get some people to come?"

"Please. I couldn't care less. I only want one person to show up but he really wants this to be lit."

"And who's the one person you want to show up?"

"You."

I grinned as I pulled up at the bus station. "Okay. Well send me the info. I just pulled up to get the twins."

"Yeah. I can't promise my speaker phone etiquette is child friendly."

I laughed. "The twins are my twenty-three-year-old cousins."

"Oh." Wesley laughed. "Still, I need to go make sure the girls haven't gotten on their grandmother's nerves. Text me later."

"I will." I hung up the call and looked around the front of the bus station until I saw Shawntay and Shawn coming out of the station. Tay, as we called her, was dragging a rolling suitcase so big I knew that something was up. I smiled when I saw Keon was with them. Key and Shawn were best friends and lovers. It was going to make for an interesting Thanksgiving. The last time Shawn brought Key to dinner, half the family came out of their mouth saying something stupid and homophobic. I had known that Shawn was gay since he was six and I had no clue why the rest of my family was so slow.

"Hey." I opened the truck door, stood on the step and waved to them. "Long time no see."

Tay squealed. "Grammy said she wasn't sure if you were going to make it."

"Whose truck did you take?"

"It belongs to a friend." I smiled at Shawn's question. Then I smiled at Key. "Hi Key. How are you?"

"I'd be fine if those two would stop plotting to destroy the planet just long enough for me to take a nap."

"No naps to be had at Grammy's." I popped the trunk so Shawn and Key could put the two huge duffle bags and suitcase they had inside. Then Key put Tay's suitcase inside. "When I left she was cussing and beating Bernard with a dish towel."

"We better hurry back. She might have upgraded to a slipper by now." Shawn chuckled. He gave me a hug before getting in the backseat behind me.

Tay got in the front seat. "Bernard is going to stop playing or I'm just going to whip his ass."

"I already called dibs on that." I groaned. Once Key was in the car, I pulled off. "He was supposed to come and get me but was playing games."

"Luckily some nice guy just let you take his truck on a holiday." Tay winked at me.

"He has another one."

"Baller." Shawn and Key called from the backseat.

Key held up a doll. "A baller with a little girl."

"He has three."

"Oh." Tay frowned her face up. "I dunno hon, you ready to be a step mommy."

"We've only been on one date. Stop moving so fast."

"One date and he is letting you drive his Escalade." Key groaned. "I should have been born a girl."

"Bae, I told you I would pay to have that done if you want."

Key sucked his teeth. "You'd miss this dick too much."

"Truth."

I laughed. "I missed you guys."

"Good cause we need to crash with you for the weekend." Tay smiled at my raised eyebrow. "Long story that I'll get into later."

"I don't have furniture."

"We got money and two air mattresses." Shawn leaned forward in the back.

"Well, y'all can help me with this party then."

"Party." Key's ears must have perked up because now he was leaning forward too.

"My friend's cousin has a club and he's throwing them a birthday but his ex is trying to sabotage it."

"You coming out of party girl retirement?" Tay started to do a little dance.

"No." I said quickly. "And now that you're here I shouldn't have to. We just need to pack the club."

"What are the details?" Tay pulled out her phone.

I tapped my phone and opened it to the flyer that Wesley sent me via text. "That's the flyer."

I glanced in the mirror and saw that all three had their phones out. I sighed, remembering when I taught them how to use social media to their advantage as soon as they graduated high school. At that point, I was paying my tuition and living expenses off the money that social media was helping me to make.

"Oh damn. He really pissed some girl named Tanika off. This bitch got him on blast." Key frowned his face up. "Did he break up with her or something."

"That's what Wesley said." I sighed.

"Fucking rookie." Tay rolled her eyes. Then they got wide.

I almost pulled over. "What?"

"His name is Doug?" She barely gave me a moment to answer. "He's one of my followers."

"Doug?" Shawn scrolled through his phone.

"D-Nice."

"Oh. Lunch dude." Shawn nodded.

"Lunch dude?" I raised my eyebrow again.

Tay smiled. "I posted on Snap that I was starving but didn't want to waste money on takeout. It was a rough couple of weeks and we were low on funds and…"

"This dude sends her a message asking for her PayPal link. She sends it and he sends her thirty dollars for lunch." Shawn finished.

"Mind you, this was a year ago." Key shook his head. "This bitch has been getting thirty dollars a week from this dude for a year."

"And I just send him thank you pictures of me stuffing my face with whatever he got me." Tay sighed. "It's his birthday. Guys, he has been feeding us for a year. We need to help him out."

"Already on it." Shawn was typing into his phone. "Hit him up and ask him if he minds us crashing his party."

"Toni, you gotta come out of retirement for this."

"No." I groaned. "I haven't even told Wesley about that part of my life. He doesn't even have social media."

"Yes he does." Key snickered. "If you consider LinkedIn a social media page."

I wanted to pull over but had to settle for Shawn reading over Key's shoulder. "What does it say?"

"This nigga fine as shit. Get it cuz." Shawn rubbed my shoulder. "He has an MBA and is Chief Operations Officer at KLM Enterprises."

"That is not on our organizational chart. He's the warehouse manager."

"Chile, did you not Google the man?" Key huffed. "Don't tell me you're fucking someone you didn't Google."

"I haven't slept with him yet." I protested.

"Good. There's still time. Tay, look this nigga up." Shawn ordered.

"Already on it." Tay was scrolling through her phone. She groaned. "The company is all secretive and shit. Why don't they post more on their website?"

“They do good business but it could be so much better. I have found so many areas to improve in just the HR side alone.” I pulled up in Grammy’s driveway.

“Wow. Doug just hit me back. He’s offering me whatever I want to come to his party.”

“Ask for his soul.”

I turned around and wacked Shawn on the arm after parking. He and Key were cracking up. “Stop it.”

“I’m asking him for just the regular rate and whatever we want to drink.”

“And two hotel rooms for after the party.” Shawn added.

“A hotel?” I turned to them.

Tay sighed. “You might be boo’d up and they haven’t had any alone time in a few days.”

I shook my head. I couldn’t knock the hustle. “Okay. Just leave me out of it.”

“Of course not.” Tay hopped out of the car and ran up the porch to hug Grammy.

I groaned. “Why is she like this?”

Key put his arm over my shoulder. “We’ve all missed you. She has missed you the most.”

I sighed. “I missed you guys too. My life is just different.”

"We get it." Shawn turned to me. "But let's have some fun for old times' sake. Plus, if you really like this Wes guy, he's going to need to know that side of you anyway. You get a couple drinks and Misty comes out with no warning and that might be an issue."

I wanted to respond but Shawn ran up to hug Grammy. I just sighed and walked up with Key.

I sat up on the couch in Grammy's basement. Key and Shawn were cuddled up on their air mattress watching a movie. Tay was in the basement bathroom taking selfies. I pulled my other phone out of my bag. Even though I had retired, I still kept my old accounts open. I simply had a second phone since my ex was desperately trying to keep me from that life. It had been great for what I needed it to be but I had long since grown weary of it.

I opened my IG and saw that not only had Shawn updated the flyer that Doug made, he added me to it. Then Tay posted it and tagged me in it. My alias was Misty. Tay used the name Bubbles and both of our names were added to the flyer. I groaned. “I told y’all…”

“No one cares what you said.” Tay called from the bathroom.

I sighed. I still had a ton of followers and was getting a lot of messages that I decided to ignore. I did post the flyer on my page and said that I was stepping out just for the night to celebrate a friend’s birthday and visit a hot club. After that, I had to go to Snap to post. Then I turned that phone back off and put it back in my bag. I was getting ready to say something when my other phone buzzed. I smiled when I saw the text from Wesley.

Wes: I’m sweet potato pie wasted.

Me: LOL. You enjoyed your dinner.

Wes: Yes. How about you? Did the fam calm down?

Me: Oh yeah. Grammy don’t take no shit when it is time to eat.

Wes: Is it tomorrow yet?

Me: Actually it is.

Wes: Ha. Okay.

Me: Hey, is it okay for me to bring my cousins up in your truck.

Wes: You can do whatever in that truck as long as it isn't illegal or sexual.

Me: Sexual?

Wes: Yeah. If I'm not a part of it nothing sexual can go down in my truck.

Me: LMAO

Wes: Can I admit something?

Me: If you want.

Wes: I took a picture of you before I woke you up this morning.

Me: Oh really.

Wes: I don't know why though. The image is plastered in my brain.

Me: You're sweet.

Wes: And you're beautiful.

Wes: Beautiful

Wes: Funny

Wes: Brilliant

Me: Stop

Wes: Why?

Me: You're making me blush

Wes: No fair. I can't see it.

I held my phone up and took a selfie of my flushed face and smile.

Me: See.

Wes: Yes, I see you with your fine ass.

Wes: So…

Me: Yes

Wes: Did you get sweet potato pie wasted?

Me: Naw.

Me: I'm macaroni and cheese wasted and will likely have an apple pie hangover in the morning

Wes: LOL

Wes: Get some sleep and text me when y'all get on the road tomorrow.

Me: Okay

Wes: You got enough gas?

Me: Yes. My cousin said he was going to fill the tank up to stop Grammy from beating him with her slipper. He gave me fifty.

Wes: I already love your Grammy.

Me: I mentioned you.

Me: I mean I had to tell her who the truck belonged to.

Wes: Ah okay

Me: She is sending you a cake for your birthday.

Wes: Aww shit

Me: LOL

Me: Go to bed.

Wes: I can't. I'm so used to being up.

Me: Same

Wes: But you need to rest if you are driving tomorrow so I'm going to let you go

Me: Okay

Wes: Don't forget…

Me: Yes. I know. Text you when we leave and text you when we get to my place

Wes: Thanks love

Wes: Good night

Me: Good night

I sat my phone down and looked over my shoulder. Tay was standing there. She sighed. "I couldn't help it. Y'all are too cute. I hope he isn't an asshole and you get to keep him."

I laughed. "I hope so too."

The drive back from Grammy's reminded me how much I missed my cousins and Key. We were always together for a few years and then I got in a relationship and they moved on with their lives. I was glad that they were doing well. Although, I knew they were all holding something back from me. I could only hope it wasn't anything serious. Shawn and Key were our bodyguards whenever Tay and I did a party or event. They made sure we got paid and didn't have to do anything we didn't want to do. When they did parties, we would make sure all the behind the scenes stuff was taken care of. Shawn and Key were both bisexual and very popular with a number of different crowds. While I never considered myself a sex worker, I had a series of short-term relationships that were very lucrative. Shawn and Key had always been down for almost anything. Something told me that Tay had started to be more open to things when I left the life.

While I enjoyed the conversation, my mind kept slipping back to what Wesley would think. Shawn and Key sat in the back, braiding and dressing every doll they found in the car. I had often wondered what little girls thought when they saw me on social media.

"Hey, pull over to that car wash. Let's get this truck washed if we gotta show up to an event in it." Key pointed.

"And stop overthinking whatever the fuck it is you are overthinking." Shawn leaned forward.

"Huh. You talking to me?" I asked.

"I'm talking to the both of you." He sucked his teeth. "We're going to get this truck washed. Then we are going to grab some food so we can take a nice power nap before show time."

"They gonna piss you at work?" Tay asked.

"No. They only do it when you get hired and if there is an issue."

"Good. I'ma need to spark up or have a brownie or something." She smiled at me.

"You good?" I looked at her when I got in the car wash line.

"Yeah. I am." She pinched my cheek. "What color hair are we wearing tonight?"

"Blue and silver."

"Yes bitch. You better show that man the amazing creature that is Misty." Key leaned forward and kissed my cheek. "He will adore her just as much as he adores you."

"How do you know he adores me?"

"You're driving his Escalade." Key sat back and huffed. "Don't act brand new."

"He has a new truck. This is the old one."

"So. Is this the one he drives all the time?" Shawn asked.

"Yes."

"So, he let you drive his baby."

I smiled as I finally understood what they were saying. "Okay. I get it."

"Good."

Chapter Five

Wesley walked through the half full club and back to Doug's office. Michelle and Fred were snuggled up on the couch. Wesley looked over at Doug, who was sitting at his desk breathing into a paper bag.

"Fuck's wrong with him?"

Michelle giggled. "He's fanboying. His favorite IG honey is actually showing up to the party."

"He thought she was just fucking with him but she has been sharing it across all her platforms."

"Wow. Well, the club is half full. Bar is crowded." Wesley sat down in the chair across from Doug.

"Is Toni coming?"

"Yeah. She just sent me a text saying she would be here in a half hour."

"Yo. She got Misty out of retirement." Doug leaned on his desk.

"Huh?"

"Bubbles got Misty out of retirement."

Wesley turned to Fred. "What is this nigga talking about?"

"Bubbles is his favorite. Misty used to be more popular than Bubbles but she retired." Michelle laughed.

"Rumor amongst the squad is that she had a man and was about that settling down life." Fred shook his head. "Don't you keep up with these things."

"No." Wesley chuckled.

"I need to smoke. I'm going to lose my shit." Doug reached in his desk drawer. Then he stopped and reached into another drawer. He pulled out a container. "Anyone want a cookie?"

"Nice." Wesley took one. "This should help me stay cool when I see Toni."

"She that pretty?" Fred asked.

"She's all the day shift guys can talk about. Someone from night shift took a picture of her and they are passing it around."

"Fucking creeps." Wesley shook his head.

"Does she have IG?" Doug asked before shoving a whole brownie in his mouth.

"Yeah." Wesley shrugged. "I don't know what it is cause I don't get on there."

"You suck." Doug mumbled through a mouthful.

Fred laughed. "So, I can go back to the sandbox and tell the guys I was at a party with an IG model."

"Yo..." Doug stood up and pointed to the screens showing images of the club. "The place is packed."

"Is that a girl standing on your bar?" Michelle walked closer.

Wesley stood up. "And another one up with the DJ."

"We better get out there." Doug closed the cookies up and headed for his office door.

Wesley shook his head. "Yeah. I gotta find Toni in that crowd."

They all walked down the hall and through the doors to the club's main room. Wesley leaned against the bar and looked up at the open DJ booth. A young girl was holding the microphone and egging the crowd on.

"Aren't y'all glad y'all came to party with us and celebrate D-Nice and Wes' birthday?" She held the mic out as the crowd roared.

The DJ pointed to Doug as he came up to the booth. "Bubbles, here's the man of the hour."

"Y'all give it up for D-Nice. He's one of my favorites." Bubbles wrapped her arms around Doug. Then she looked at the crowd. "Yo, someone tag ole girl and tell her I said thank you."

Wesley noticed there was a guy in all black not too far from where Bubbles was standing. He wondered if that was her bodyguard. Then he saw another guy, who seemed to be wearing the same slacks and shirt standing two seats from him.

"Aye, Misty. Did you find the other birthday boy?" Bubbles asked.

Wesley turned around and saw that the girl on the bar was standing behind him. He faced her and looked up. She was wearing black leather thigh high boots, tight booty shorts, and a shirt that had so many slices in it he could see the lace pattern of her bra even if it didn't sparkle in the club lights. It was her hips that caught his attention. He knew that shape. Even with the blue and silver wig on, he knew that body.

The girl, Misty, slowly dropped into a squat in front of him and she smiled. "Hey cutie."

"Toni…"

She put her finger over his lips. "I'm Misty, at least for as long as we're in here."

He kissed her fingers. Then he looked to his right. "Is that your bodyguard?"

"Yes."

"I don't want no smoke when I touch you."

Misty smiled and kissed Wesley. He grabbed her by her waist and helped her off the bar. Then Misty led him up to the VIP section.

She stopped at the top of the steps and turned. "Key, this is Wes. Wes, this is Key."

Wesley shook his hand. Key had a firm grip that solidified in Wesley's mind that Key went to the gym way more often than he did. However, Key gave him a nod of approval and walked to stand over near the railing. Wesley took Misty over to Michelle and Fred.

"Misty, this is my sister Michelle and her husband Fred. Guys, this is Misty."

"But…" Michelle got quiet when Fred whispered something in her ear. Then she smiled. "Nice to meet you Misty. Thanks for saving the party."

"Anything for Wes."

Wesley spent the rest of the night telling his dick to chill. Between watching Misty take selfies and videos, dance, and having her dance in his lap he wasn't sure how much longer he could stretch the tiny bit of self-control he had left. He knew that Misty was Antoinette. He also knew this side of Antoinette turned him on even more than the side he had known before. He wasn't even sure how that was possible. She was the same but she was totally different.

Fred leaned over to him. "Aye, you seem to be liking this side of her."

"Yo. If we were in Vegas right now, I would drag her out of here and marry her."

"Word?"

"Fuck yeah."

Fred laughed. "Michelle said y'all hadn't…"

"We haven't. I'm resisting the urge to straight caveman toss her ass over my shoulder right now."

"Doug said he only had them until one and it's about that time now." Fred pointed to his watch and then looked at Michelle. "I'm about to go try and make you an uncle. Happy Birthday. Hopefully I see you before I head to the airport."

Wesley shook his hand and gave him a hug. "Not likely. Take care of yourself."

"You know it."

Fred and Michelle left. Wesley sat back and watched Misty. She was taking pictures with a few of the other girls up in VIP. Then he saw Bubbles walk over to her with Key and the other guy. Misty led them over to Wesley. She straddled his lap.

"Wes, is Doug cool or am I going to have to kill him?"

"Huh?"

"Bubbles wants to leave with him… just to talk." Misty rolled her eyes and glanced back at Bubbles. "Key and Shawn want to know if he is good."

"He hurts her and I will kill him myself. He already knows this." Wesley paused and flagged down Doug. "Yo D, where are you trying to take her?"

"To talk and chill." Doug looked at Key and Shawn. "We could just go to the hotel. I got two rooms. They are next door to each other."

Misty nodded. Wesley raised an eyebrow at Doug. "Don't make me have to kill you yo."

"I know. I know. We're good."

Wesley watched the four of them leave the VIP section. Then he turned to see Misty watching the area. He looked down and watched her chest rise and fall with her breathing. He looked further down and looked at her sitting in his lap. His dick instantly hardened.

Misty turned to look at him. "Oh. You must be ready to go too."

"I was ready the minute I saw you."

"I'm glad you were able to hold it together this long." She giggled. Then she stood up. "Let's go so I can take care of that for you."

"Girl you ain't said nothing but a word." Wesley followed Misty out of the club. They went over to his truck and he helped her in. He looked at her when he got in and had to adjust the driver's seat. "I should let you drive."

"I have had way too much of way too much to drive."

"Okay." Wesley chuckled. "Back to your place."

She looked at him. "Bubbles has my keys."

"My place it is." Wesley started the truck. He glanced over at Misty and she smiled at him. He wasn't sure how he got so lucky but he decided to thank every deity he could think of on the ride home just to make sure he gave credit to the right one.

"You went to the barbershop." Misty reached her hand across the truck and rubbed the side of Wesley's face.

"Yeah. I had to look nice for you."

"For me?"

"Yeah. Had to show you that I clean up nice."

"I knew you cleaned up nice." Misty traced her fingers down the fresh shape up and she began to play with his beard. "We might not make it to your house."

"Huh?"

Misty took off her seatbelt and leaned over to kiss Wesley on his neck. "I don't think I can fight it any longer."

Wesley's dick got rock hard as she whispered in his ear. He decided it was best to take a detour as Misty began to open his pants. "Ma'am."

"Wes…" Misty giggled and continued to kiss Wesley on his neck.

Wesley was able to pull off and park the truck safely before Misty got his pants open and his dick out of his boxer briefs. He turned to her and kissed her. Her tongue immediately parted his lips and began to play with his tongue. Wesley slipped his hands down to her hips and pushed down the leather spandex shorts she had on. Misty sat back and pushed them all the way down. After kicking them off, she climbed into Wesley's lap.

Wesley chuckled when she pressed the button on the seat, causing him to lean all the way back. "Figured out how the truck works?"

"Yes." Misty pulled the t-shirt over her head. She bent down to kiss him softly and sat back up with a condom in her hand.

"Prepared?"

"I'm always prepared for whatever. Hazard of my former lifestyle." Misty opened the condom and slowly slid it on Wesley.

Her grip caused him to groan. "You sure you don't want to wait until…"

"I need you inside me." Misty lifted up and then slowly sat back down, allowing his hardness to slip inside of her.

"Oh shit girl." Wesley moaned.

Misty moaned as she tried to get all of him in on the first try. Wesley pulled her down and captured her next moan in a kiss. He slid down in the seat a little more. Then he held her hips and guided her as he stroked deeper inside of her. Soon Misty was riding him and nibbling on his bottom lip while moans escaped her lips. Wesley grabbed her ass and enjoyed the ride. Misty knew exactly how to work her hips and pull him close to orgasm. When he felt himself ready to pop he reached around and began to massage her clit. He didn't realize a few touches would throw her straight into an orgasm that had her crying out.

"Wes, baby, yes."

Her walls tightened and he pounded deep into her as he climaxed. He held her close through the aftershocks. They stayed like that for a while. Wesley wasn't sure how long but he was so comfortable he didn't want to attempt to move her.

Then Misty sat up and looked at him. "Are you upset with me?"

“No baby.” Wesley pulled her back close to him and kissed her lips.

“I can explain…”

“Shhhh…” He kissed her again. “We can talk later.”

“Okay.” She kissed him one more time before climbing back over to the passenger side of the car.

Wesley fixed his pants and then sat his seat back up. “You okay?”

Misty pulled her shorts back on, struggling to get them over her hips. “I’m a little bigger than when I bought these.”

“You look fucking amazing in them though.”

She smiled and looked out the window at the house that seemed to be under construction. “Where are we?”

“This is my land.”

“The house you’re having built?”

“Yes.”

“Wow. It looks nice.”

“One day, in the daylight, I will show you around.”

“I’d like that.” She smiled at him.

Wesley started the car. “Now, we can go back to my place.”

Misty gazed out the window as Wesley drove. After a few minutes, she fell asleep. Wesley went back to thanking every deity he could think of.

I woke up and had only a few moments to figure out where I was and find the bathroom. I threw up what felt like the entire contents of my stomach. When I finally felt like I was finished, I sat down on the floor of the bathroom. My mind ran over all of the things I had ingested before going to the party. Then I remembered Tay giving me a pill when I had begun to freak out about Wesley finding out about my past. I tried to stand up and had to lean on the counter. I rinsed my mouth out and flushed the toilet. My body began to shake as I tried to splash water on my face. My vision got blurry and I knocked over a few things while trying to turn the water off.

Wesley appeared in the doorway. He was wearing his boxer briefs and a concerned look. "Babe, what did you take?"

I reached out for him and he caught me before I fell. I looked up at him as he pulled me into his arms. "Tay gave me a molly so I wouldn't punk out of coming. I was scared about you seeing the other side of me."

"Shit. Okay." Wesley took me over to the shower and turned the water on. He took his boxer briefs off and got in the shower with me.

"I'm sorry."

"Babe, it's okay. Calm down and breathe." He leaned against the shower wall and held me so the water was running over my back.

It took a while for my body to stop shaking. "This isn't as bad as I have been."

"Really?"

I looked up at him and then immediately looked away. He tilted my head so we made eye contact again. I bit my lip. "At one point I got really bad and had to go stay with Grammy for three months."

"And then you stopped?"

"The drugs, yes. Well I would smoke every now and again. But no pills. I was trying to set a better example for Tay but I think I failed."

Wesley kissed me on the forehead. "I was told you retired."

"I did. Just before I met my ex, I had decided I wanted to do something different."

"So, no more Misty."

"I like being Toni. I still get looks and guys saying crazy shit to me though."

"As fine as you are, men are going to get stupid around you. Especially ones that ain't got good sense to know you might not like it."

"I like how you approached me." I smiled at him.

"Seriously? I was awkward as fuck."

"I liked it."

Wesley smiled at me. "Well I'm a new fan of Misty. Lawd."

I giggled.

"But I'm falling hard for you Toni."

"You like my different sides."

"Oh, fuck yeah. That pushed me over the edge."

I reached up and put my arms over his shoulders. Wesley leaned down and kissed me on my forehead. "Can we go back to bed?"

"Yeah. You aren't shaking anymore." Wesley turned the water off. He got out and then wrapped me in a towel. Then he picked the things up off the floor I had knocked over.

"I need that." I pointed to the mouthwash. I rinsed my mouth out and then kicked Wesley out of the bathroom so I could pee.

He handed me a shirt when I walked back into the huge space. He had a studio apartment. The kitchen was a room by itself and on the other side by a door. He smiled at me. "I know you don't like clothes but just in case."

"In case?"

"I swear I lock every lock in here but those girls somehow find a way in when they want to get in."

I giggled and put the shirt on. Then I paused. "If you want to take me home, I can text Tay and get my keys."

"Naw. I want to curl up in bed and wrap my arms around you. I wanna sleep for as long as I am allowed to just like that." Wesley pulled me over to the bed. "I need to rub on that booty until I pass out."

Chapter Six

I was sitting up and scanning my phone, looking at all the videos and pictures that were posted about the party. I had both phones in my lap. The Misty phone was where I was looking at all the evening's footage. On my other phone I was in a group chat with Tay, Shawn, and Key. Shawn started it to make sure Tay and I were okay. We both sent selfies. Tay was in the hotel bed and she sent a picture of Doug. He was still in his clothes and laying across the foot of the bed. She had tossed a cover over him and it reminded me of Wesley at my house a few nights earlier. Key said he could see Wesley's hand holding my boob through the shirt I was wearing. I had taken my picture before I sat up. Shawn and Key were still in the hotel room next to where Tay was. They were just too lazy to get up and check on her. We were all cracking jokes about the party footage when Tay sent me a separate text.

Tay: I'm sorry about giving you that pill. Are you okay?

Me: Yeah. I am okay.

Tay: I'm really sorry. I was trying to help and then I realized last night that I shouldn't have cause you quit and…

Tay: I'm sorry

Me: It's okay. I am fine. I talked to Wesley. He got me in the shower. I puked my life away but I am good.

Tay: Was he upset about you being Misty.

Me: Naw. He likes her a lot.

Tay: LOL. He's a freak.

Me: I feel like I can be myself though

Tay: That is so important

Me: What did you and Doug talk about?

Tay: Stuff

Me: Tay…

Tay: He saw some snaps I had posted and then deleted. He was worried about me but I told him I'm fine.

Me: What is going on?

Tay: We'll talk about it later.

Me: We better

Tay: Enjoy your boo. Doug seems to be waking up. I'ma see if he wants to get some food.

Me: Text me if y'all get back to the apartment before me

Me: One of y'all has my keys

Tay: Shawn has them

I put my phone down when I heard a key turn in the door near the kitchen. Then three girls came into the space. They didn't see me at first.

"Shove the key in your pocket." One said.

The youngest looked at me and smiled. "Hi."

I smiled back. "Hi."

"Uh oh." The one with the key froze. "We didn't know daddy had company."

"Daddy never has company." The little one walked closer.

"Are you Misty?" The tallest one took a few steps closer. "I know you from IG."

I nodded. "My name is really Toni."

The one with the key sighed. "I'm so glad. I overheard grandma telling Aunt Michelle that she thought daddy had a thing for you and I hoped he didn't mess it up."

I covered my mouth as I laughed. "No. He didn't."

"Daddy's trending." The little one handed me her tablet.

I blushed when I saw the picture of me dancing on his lap. "Oh wow."

"You look beautiful." The tallest stood next to the little one. "I showed my mom a picture of you once and she said she liked that you had curves and posted pictures without makeup."

I smiled. "I tried to be as real as possible on that account."

"What's on your locked account?"

"It's locked for a reason." I raised my eyebrow at that one. "How old are you?"

"I'm nine and my name is Carly."

"I'm Camryn. I'm ten."

I glanced at the little one. "You must be Corrine? Your dad said you like Wonder Woman more than I do."

"I'm switching cause Black Panther is coming out and I heard there are girls in it. Daddy's going to get me a book about it."

Carly rolled her eyes. "She's eight."

"So, you don't do the IG stuff anymore?" Camryn asked.

"Nope. I work in Human Resources now." I glanced at Wesley. He was still knocked out.

"Daddy won't wake up unless we jump on the bed or turn the television up loud." Camryn smiled. "I want to work in an office like my grandmother. She said one day I could have her job."

"That sounds exciting." I smiled at her. "I took classes in college and decided I really like HR."

"Are you good at it?" Corrine carefully climbed on the bed. When Wesley didn't budge, her sisters did the same.

"I think so. My boss likes my work."

"Is that a wig?" Corrine pointed to my hair.

"Corry, that's rude." Camryn scolded.

"It's okay. I mean it is blue hair." I undid the two clips holding my wig in place and took it off. I hadn't taken the time to even braid my hair. It was just pulled back in a tight ponytail and pinned up. I took out the ponytail and additional clips. "See. This is me."

"Your hair is pretty. Do you have a perm? Daddy won't let me get one." Carly frowned.

"Yes. I have a perm. It's a pain. You should really wait until you are older to get it. It's a lot of work to keep your hair healthy."

"Oh, I don't wanna do work." She groaned.

We all giggled. Corrine looked at me. "We're taking daddy to dinner for his birthday. You should come."

"Oh no sweetie. You guys should have him all to yourselves for that dinner." I smiled at her.

"You could come out with us another time maybe?"

I looked at Camryn and Carly's hopeful eyes. I had never been around the kids of any of the guys I dated before. It was all new territory for me and I was unsure of what to say. I nodded. "If your daddy says it's okay then we can all go out another time."

"You gonna put up with my daddy for long enough?" Corrine asked.

This time we all giggled, louder than before, and Wesley lifted his head and looked at us.

The girls all began to sing Happy Birthday to him. He glanced at me and I smiled. When they were finished he raised his eyebrow.

"How did y'all get in here?"

We all shrugged.

"Daddy, we got reservations in two hours. You gotta get up." Corrine nudged him.

"Okay. I'm up."

"You're trending daddy." Carly giggled.

Wesley raised his eyebrow again and looked at me. I looked away. He groaned. "Y'all go and get ready. Did your aunt and grandmother leave?"

"Yes." They all chimed in.

"Camryn, you're in charge. Make sure you and your sisters get dressed and then sit and wait for me in the living room."

"Yes sir." Camryn got up first.

"Daddy, we invited Toni but she said she will come another time." Carly frowned.

"Sounds like a plan." Wesley sat up.

"Daddy, you have blotches like auntie Michelle had this morning. Did you two use the same soap?"

I blushed while Camryn and Carly burst into a fit of giggles. Wesley covered his face with his hands for a second. Then he looked at Corrine. "Yes sweetie. We used the same soap. Now go use your soap on your body."

Camryn took Corrine by the arm and they followed Carly out the door, shutting it behind them.

I traced my fingers over one of the passion marks I left on his neck. "Sorry."

Wesley shook his head. "Pat has already started talking to them about boys and sex but Corrine will likely be my naive little girl for a while longer."

"I wasn't expecting them to..."

Wesley kissed me and I forgot what I was going to say. Then he looked at me. “You know, you’re welcome to come to dinner with us tonight.”

“No. That is your time with your girls.” I tried to get out of bed but he wrapped his arms around me and pulled me close. “Wes…”

“I do not want to let you go.” He nuzzled his face in my neck.

“I need to go home and make sure my cousins are okay. I have a paper to finish and it isn’t like I’m running away.”

“I certainly hope not.”

“I can order a ride to pick me up and…”

“Nope. Just take my truck.”

“Wesley, I’m not taking your truck.”

He sighed. “Then we can drop you off on our way.”

“Wes…”

“We’re going to pass your place anyway.” He began to kiss me softly on my clavicle.

I sighed. “Okay. Fine.”

“Good.”

“I’m going to shower. You should go upstairs and check on the girls.”

"Yeah, that middle one will still be in what she had on if I don't go make her change."

I kissed him and then broke free of his grasp. "Can you get my bag out of your truck first?"

Wesley stood up and walked over to the sofa. He carried my bag over to the bed. "I figured you might need it."

"Thank you." I smiled.

Wesley pulled on shorts and a shirt and then headed upstairs. I went into the bathroom and took a shower. When I came out, he was back downstairs checking his phone. He took his clothes and went into the bathroom. I was already half dressed, unsure of who would be in his room when I came out, so I just needed to pull on my sweatshirt. Then I sat on his couch.

Carly came downstairs a few minutes later. She didn't say a word but held out a brush and a bottle of grease. I smiled. Her hair did not survive her shower.

"Come on over here so I can fix you up."

"Thank you. Camryn brushes too hard." Carly came over and sat on the floor in between my legs.

"How do you want me to do it?"

"Something pretty."

I thought for a moment and then decided to do four braids. Carly had a good amount of hair to work with and it was hard to comb through. I remembered how Grammy used to do my hair. I simply took my time and was as gentle as possible. Wesley came out of the bathroom while I was on the last braid. I glanced at him and he smiled. Then he walked to his closet to find a shirt to put on.

"All finished." I patted Carly on the shoulder.

She hopped up and ran to the mirror. "Oh, this is pretty. Daddy, doesn't my hair look pretty?"

"Yes it does."

"Thank you Toni."

"You're welcome."

"Go get your sisters so we can go." Wesley pointed to the door.

I got up off the couch. "Has she ever worn braids?"

"Her mother was asking if I would pay for that. I heard it pulls their hair out."

"Not if you go to the right place." I raised my eyebrow. "Does their mother have a place in mind?"

"The place she goes."

"Is her hair falling out?"

Wesley sighed. "No."

"Oh. Okay." I decided not to say anything else. I didn't want to tread too far into his relationship with his daughters or his ex.

The girls came running down the steps. Camryn had a purse on. "Daddy, we're ready."

"Can we take the new truck?" Corrine danced.

"Yes." Wesley winked at me.

I looked away and chuckled. I was certain he still had to clean the truck we were in the night before. I followed the girls outside to Wesley's brand-new black Suburban.

Camryn turned to me. "You can ride up front because daddy says I'm still not old enough."

"Well thank you." I smiled at her.

Wesley shook his head and opened the doors for us. Before I got in, he leaned down to me. "Do I have to take you home?"

"Yes. But you can call me when the girls go to bed tonight."

He groaned. "I guess that will work."

I laughed.

Wesley was just getting ready to call Antoinette and see what she was doing when he got a call from work. He was sitting at the kitchen counter, having just finished cleaning up from a late dinner.

"Man, I know you're off until tomorrow but I don't want you coming in here pissed." James sounded stressed.

"What's up?"

"It was all jokes and fun yesterday and I thought it wouldn't be an issue but they still on that bullshit today. I don't need you losing your temper. We're itching on five months since that last thing happened."

"James, what's the problem?"

"We aren't going to have the trucks ready for tomorrow morning."

"What?" Wesley groaned. "Why the fuck aren't y'all gonna be ready? We finished half of it Wednesday night."

"I let some shit slide yesterday that I shouldn't have and now they trying to let that shit roll today."

"I'll be there in a half hour." Wesley hung up the phone.

"What's wrong?"

Wesley turned to see his mother pouring herself a glass of wine. "Problem at work."

"Anything I need to know about?"

Wesley shook his head. "Nope. Except there is likely to be mandatory overtime tonight."

Mrs. Scott sighed. "Wesley…"

"I don't want to hear it right now mom. Fuss at me tomorrow." Wesley got up and headed to the steps that led to his apartment.

He arrived at the warehouse and it seemed like the entire mood shifted as soon as he walked in the doors. All the laughing and joking stopped. He saw people hurrying back to their stations and trying to look busy. He walked to his office and opened the door to go inside. Then he stopped and pressed the button on the intercom system.

"Mandatory overtime. No one leaves until the trucks are done."

James came in his office and shut the door just as Wesley was sitting down. "Um…"

"Pull the girls upstairs and anyone else. Boss lady is going to kill me if those trucks don't leave on time in the morning. I'm not dying alone." Wesley turned on his computer and then looked up at James, who hadn't said another word. "What?"

"Okay. So, I know I shouldn't have let them start with the jokes. It was pretty tame for a while but today it's crazy."

"What jokes?"

"About Antoinette."

Wesley raised his eyebrow. "Excuse me?"

"Someone outed her as a social media model named Misty and they were cracking jokes yesterday. I told them I was writing anyone up who had their phones out and that cut most of the noise down. I don't know what happened between today and yesterday but..." James paused. "You're not going to be happy."

"Well since we already know that perhaps you should just tell me the rest."

James handed him a folded-up sheet of paper. "I got this from the guys on the loading dock. They said a supervisor printed it for them. They wouldn't tell me which one."

Wesley opened the paper and his stomach tightened. It was a picture from his birthday party. The picture was of Misty dancing in his lap. There was also a picture of Antoinette, the one from her ID picture. Underneath both it read: *Guess who's giving lap dances for promotions*. Wesley sat the paper down and smoothed out the creases from the fold as he tried to calm down.

"Wes..."

"I want every supervisor in here in the conference room in twenty minutes."

"You gonna calm down in twenty minutes?"

"They better pray I do."

James nodded and left the office. Wesley leaned back in his seat and took several deep breaths. He heard James over the loudspeaker calling all overnight shift staff to the warehouse floor. Then James called for a management meeting in fifteen minutes. He picked up his phone and dialed a number quickly.

"Security."

"Hey, who's in charge down there tonight?"

"Hey Wesley. Timothy was actually on his way to your office about an email he sent you."

"Good. Thanks." Wesley hung up the phone and waited. The security office was only down the hall so there was a knock on his door in a matter of minutes. "Come in."

Timothy stuck his head in. "You flip out yet?"

"What the fuck is this shit?" Wesley handed him the paper.

Timothy sighed. "Listen. That's the easiest issue to deal with."

"Is it? Is it really?"

"You didn't check your email?"

"No."

Timothy opened up his laptop and turned it to face Wesley. On the tape was one of his supervisors having sex in a warehouse hallway with a woman.

"Man, turn that shit off." Wesley leaned back and groaned loudly.

Timothy closed the laptop. "That particular email you have was sent by the girl in HR, Shauna. She's so fucking stupid she sent it to the night guard."

"On the company email."

"Yes."

Wesley rolled his eyes. "And this video?"

"That is the other girl in HR. Her name is…"

"Keisha."

"Yes. Apparently, she and David have been screwing all over the building but this is the first time we got it on tape.

David was a big part of the jokes last night, which I thought was really ironic."

"Why?"

"They are saying that Diane is really running a brothel up there." Timothy stepped back when Wesley shot him a nasty glance. "Don't shoot the messenger. Antoinette didn't do anything wrong. They hate her because she is beautiful and smart."

"And they're clearly neither." Wesley shook his head. "My mother is going to lose her shit."

"What do you want to do?"

"I'm going to leave that to her. I'm trying to hold my temper together. I have to talk to my managers about this delayed shipment." Wesley handed him the paper. "Can you find out who printed that?"

"I will get the night IT guy right on it."

"Thanks."

"Should I go to this meeting with you?"

"Naw." Wesley got up and walked to the door. Then he turned back to Timothy. "Maybe."

Timothy chuckled. "Okay. Let's go."

Wesley and Timothy headed down the hallway to the warehouse conference room. James was standing outside the door. All three walked in the room at the same time. It was as if someone turned off a stereo. All the laughter and talking stopped when Wesley walked into the room.

He stood at the head of the conference room table. "Why is my shipment going to be late?"

The room was quiet. Finally, one of the supervisors spoke up. "We were a little lax on goals last night."

"And everyone will pay for that tonight." Wesley looked around the room. "No one leaves until the shipment is ready or they hit twelve hours on the clock. Anybody who clocks out before that will be written up."

The supervisors all nodded.

Wesley sighed. "Get back to work."

Everyone began to get up. David leaned over to another supervisor. "Man, somebody call Toni and get her in here. Wesley needs to relax."

"What the fuck did you just say?" Wesley looked at David.

"I mean… I'm just saying." David spoke louder. "None of us blame you. She is fine as fuck. No one in this room can say they haven't dreamt of fucking her. I'm just hoping I can afford her when you are done with her."

Wesley tried to take a few deep breaths. He felt someone touch his shoulder and he tried hard to control his temper but the smirk on David's face set him off. Wesley popped David in the mouth so quickly the other guys jumped back. Before Timothy could get over to them, Wesley had David by the throat and slammed him against the wall.

"Nigga you really need to learn when to shut the fuck up." James grabbed one of Wesley's arms and Timothy grabbed the other. They had to tug several times before Wesley let David go.

"James, take Wesley to my office and keep him there." Timothy ordered.

"Anybody else got some slick shit to say about my girlfriend?" Wesley looked around the room. All the other supervisors shook their head.

James opened the door to the conference room. Wesley walked with James down the hall. He walked just past the security office door and out a door that led to the outside. James went with him. Wesley paced outside and took in the crisp, fresh air. After a few minutes he looked over at James.

"You calm?"

"Slightly."

James sat down on the steps. "A few of us looked like we were going to smack him but you were just too quick with yours."

Wesley paced some more.

"Yo, I hate to be you tomorrow though."

Wesley groaned. "My mother is going to kick my ass."

I woke up Monday afternoon to my phone buzzing across the nightstand.

"Hello."

"Antoinette, hi. I'm sorry if I woke you."

I sat up at the sound of Diane's voice. "It's fine. My alarm was set to go off in a few minutes anyway. What's up?"

"We need you to come in early."

"What time?"

"As soon as possible."

I sighed. "Okay. It'll take me about an hour and a half to get there."

"That should be fine. Thank you. I'll meet you in my office when you get here."

"Okay. See you then."

I sat my phone back down and did a yawn and stretch combination that really just made me want to curl back up in bed. Then I picked up my phone again to see if I got a text from Wesley. He had said he would call me the night before but simply sent a text saying that he had to go into work. I hadn't heard from him since then. I sighed when I still didn't have a text or missed call.

There was a text from Shawn letting me know that they had made it to New York. My cousins spent a day at the apartment with me. Tay never did tell me what was going on. She preferred to camp out on the air mattress and watch television in my room. I decided it was best to let it go. Tay had always been extremely emotional and I didn't want to put her in a bad place. Key and Shawn joked me for not having furniture and they cooked us food when they weren't on my floor watching television with Tay.

They left early that morning, catching a cab to the bus station. Shawn said they had a few events lined up in New York and would try to come back around Christmas time. Key fussed at me to message them and tell them how I was doing. I fussed back for the same thing. I enjoyed having them close again and missed them immediately after they were gone. They were the only people I knew were my friends no matter what happened, and we had already been through a lot.

A knot formed in the pit of my stomach when I got to work. As soon as I went through the security checkpoint, Timothy met me. He was the night security manager.

"A bit early for you, isn't it?" I smiled at him.

"I can say the same for you." He looked at his watch. It was just three o'clock. I usually didn't start my shift until five at the earliest.

"Yeah. Diane asked me to come in early."

"I know. Allow me to take you to her." Timothy motioned in the direction of the elevators that led to the administrative side of the building. I had never been on that side and was nervous as to why I was going over there. Timothy was quiet in the elevator. He smiled at me when the doors opened to the top floor. We got to a set of double glass doors and he stopped. "Wait here for a moment. I'll be right back."

I did as I was asked, choosing to look around at how nicely the area was decorated. It was clear that our CEO was a woman with really good taste. Either that or she hired a decorator with really good taste. Instead of the boring old beige and blues, maroon and cream were the neutrals. Green was the color used to add a bit of pop to the design.

"Well if it isn't the famous Ms. Antoinette." A guy I had never seen before came down the hallway towards the double doors.

"Excuse me?" I said, being careful to watch my tone since I had no clue who this man was. I did know that he was looking at me like I was naked when I was clearly wearing an oversized sweater, black slacks, and slip resistant shoes.

"You know, I have a birthday coming up and…"

I hadn't noticed the double doors open but Greg Saunders came out and walked over to the guy. His entire demeanor was different than I had ever seen. His shoulders were hunched forward and he had a scowl on his face. He didn't touch the guy but his presence caused the guy to back against the wall and stand on his toes, as if trying to climb away.

Greg looked at me. "Did he say what I heard him say?"

"Um…" I didn't know how to answer.

"Greg, I was joking."

"I don't like jokes like that. I don't find that shit funny." Greg shook his head. "My mother called a meeting ten minutes ago. You're late."

"I was on a conference call."

"You were told the meeting was urgent. That means you drop everything and bring your ass."

"Gregory."

I turned and looked at the woman standing in the doorway. There weren't very many pictures of Mrs. Scott around the building but I recognized her from the one she allowed on the website.

"Yes ma'am."

"Can we not?"

Gregory backed up. "Yes ma'am."

"Mr. Ingram, you have missed the meeting. You can report to Mrs. Lawson's office and she will bring you up to speed." Mrs. Scott stared at the guy when he didn't move immediately. "Mr. Ingram, I advise you to move quickly.

From what I have heard you're still in your probationary period."

He turned and hurried down the hall. When he was out of ear shot, Greg turned to Mrs. Scott. "Ma…"

"Make a decision on him and text your sister. I'm not in the mood." She turned and smiled at me. "Ms. Bailey, please join me in my office."

Greg smiled at me and held the glass door open so that I could follow his mother down the hall to her giant office. I glanced behind me when he shut the door. Greg did not join us. I took a deep breath and turned to face Mrs. Scott.

"Please, have a seat." She waited until I sat down to sit down. "Okay, I'm not one to beat around the bush. You'll learn that about me. I first want to go over your thought process behind these organizational changes you are suggesting."

"Well…"

"And please just be straight with me. No need to sugarcoat anything."

I nodded and went over all the changes I was suggesting and why. When I finished, I made eye contact with her again. "Diane said that some of this was how the company used to be and I think it worked. I think you guys changed too much. Putting some of the things back the way they were will be a great move for the company."

Mrs. Scott was quiet for a moment. She was clearly thinking, spinning and rocking slightly in her chair. Then she nodded. "Okay. Well we're going to make those changes and see how things go."

"Really?"

"Yes." She sighed. "Now, to the next reason why you are here. I need to know how thick your skin is."

"Excuse me?"

She sat a paper in front of me that took my breath away. It was a printed-out email with a picture of me dancing with Wesley at his birthday party. There was also a copy of my work ID photo. I looked away before even reading the words because I could guess what they said. Mrs. Scott took the paper back. "Your former coworker thought it was cute to circulate this on company email. That's why she is your former coworker. Your other coworker was let go for inappropriate conduct on the job. I want to promote you to our night shift HR Supervisor. Diane is being promoted to the Director of HR and will supervise the day shift staff. Here's the deal, not only are you going to start with no staff you are also going to have to deal with this. We have…"

Mrs. Scott stopped talking when her office door opened. Wesley came in her office and stretched out on the couch.

"Wesley…"

"Look, I was here until seven this morning. Then I had to come back and talk to security and police and I'm exhausted and not in the mood. I promised Toni that our relationship was not going to affect her job." He looked at Mrs. Scott. "Ma, please don't make a liar out of me."

"Boy if you don't hush." She rolled her eyes and looked at me. "You'll learn he's a grumpy ass fool when he's sleepy."

"That's when he starts yelling on the warehouse floor?"

"Exactly." She nodded.

I smiled at Wesley.

"Wes, I'm offering her Diane's old job if she is willing to deal with the aftermath of her simple ass old coworker."

"Oh." Wesley let his head fall back on the pillow.

I turned to her. "I didn't know he was your son too."

"We all have different last names."

"Her favorite hobby is getting married."

"Boy, I will smack you in front of your girlfriend. Ask Greg about that." Mrs. Scott rolled her eyes again. "You best take a nap while Toni and I get some work done before I end up embarrassing you."

"Knock knock."

I looked up and saw Wesley walking over to my cubicle. "Hi. You just woke up?"

"Naw. I woke up an hour ago. I went down to the warehouse to make sure we don't have a repeat of last night."

"Did Mrs. Scott finally leave?"

"Her note said she left at seven. I need a couch like hers in my office."

I laughed. "No, you don't."

Wesley leaned on my file cabinet. "I'm sorry I didn't tell you she was my mother."

"It's okay." I smiled at him.

"I feel like I should have told you but we were moving slow and…"

"Wes, it's okay." I reached for his hand.

"You aren't moving to an office?"

"I am. I just got distracted looking over resumes for new HR clerks."

"Oh." Wesley pulled my hand up to his lips.

"Is that allowed?"

He chuckled. "That is about all that is allowed."

"Diane said the rumor was you punched someone."

"I might have." Wesley rolled his eyes.

"You can't do that."

"He said some slick shit."

"That guy, Mr. Ingram, started to say slick shit and I thought Greg was going to hit him. I have never seen him like that."

"We do share a mother so…" Wesley chuckled. Then he looked at me. "Are you going to honestly be able to deal with this? My mother scared the shit out of most of the people here, threatening to research their personal lives if they felt that was what should be discussed at work. But that isn't going to fix everything."

I sighed. "Wes, I have dealt with looks and stares since before puberty. I had to deal with similar shit in college. Every job I ever had there was some shit at some point. I like working here."

"Cause I work here?"

I laughed. "You're a bonus. I liked it before I started liking you."

"Fair enough." Wesley yawned. "So, you've been here eight hours already so I think I should take you home."

"But..."

"I killed the overtime budget for the rest of the month."

I giggled. "Okay."

"Until they switch you to salary, I need you to clock out." Wesley pointed to my computer.

"Did you eat?"

"Naw."

"There is still some chicken I fried for my cousins to take with them on the bus." I logged off my computer.

"Oh, that sounds like a plan."

As I put some things in my bag, to work on the next afternoon, I thought about something Mrs. Scott had said. "Wes, you know your mom called me your girlfriend."

"Did it bother you?"

"No."

"So, you'll be my girlfriend?"

I giggled.

"I don't have to write you a note?"

"No. You don't have to write me a note. I'm happy to be your girlfriend."

"So, you'll help me decorate this house."

"I'll help your girls help you decorate your house."

Wesley helped me put my coat on. "Okay."

"That should be their job. I'm sure they have great ideas."

"And maybe I can get a visit from Misty again." Wesley took my bag and led me to the elevator. "Not too often cause she's wild and I'm old but…"

I laughed. "Maybe after some chicken and potatoes you can meet Toni and compare."

"Oh, now that really sounds like the plan."

Other works by Turtleberry

Are You Okay?

Nobody's Somebody

Sweet Turtleberry Jam Volume One

These Women Book One

These Women Book Two

These Women Book Three

Happily Ever After

Sweet Turtleberry Jam Volume Two

Catching Evie

Needs To Be Met

Love Unexpected

Lena's Chance At Love

www.sweetturtleberry.com

www.ingramcontent.com/pod-product-compliance
Lightning Source LLC
LaVergne TN
LVHW012116170826
845678LV00014BA/2962

* 9 7 9 8 8 4 8 7 1 4 4 9 4 *